CAPTAIN FACT
SPACE ADVENTURE

Read all the adventures
starring the fact-astic

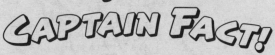

#1 Captain Fact Space Adventure
#2 Captain Fact Dinosaur Adventure

CAPTAIN FACT SPACE ADVENTURE

by
Knife & Packer

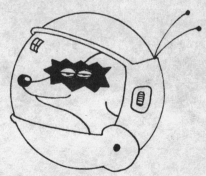

SCHOLASTIC INC.
New York Toronto London Auckland Sydney
Mexico City New Delhi Hong Kong Buenos Aires

ISBN 0-439-80691-7

Copyright © 2004 by Knife and Packer. All rights reserved.
Published by Scholastic Inc., 557 Broadway, New York, NY 10012,
by arrangement with Hyperion Books for Children, an imprint of
Disney Children's Book Group, LLC. SCHOLASTIC and associated logos
are trademarks and/or registered trademarks of Scholastic Inc.

12 11 10 9 8 7 6 5 4 3 2 1   5 6 7 8 9 10/0

Printed in the U.S.A.   40

First Scholastic printing, September 2005

This book is set in 12/16 Excelsior.

CONTENTS

STARR

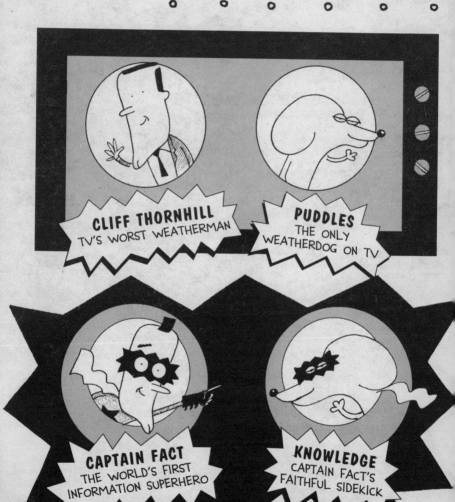

CLIFF THORNHILL
TV'S WORST WEATHERMAN

PUDDLES
THE ONLY
WEATHERDOG ON TV

CAPTAIN FACT
THE WORLD'S FIRST
INFORMATION SUPERHERO

KNOWLEDGE
CAPTAIN FACT'S
FAITHFUL SIDEKICK

NG . . .

LUCY
HEAD OF MAKEUP AND
CLIFF'S BEST FRIEND

THE BOSS
HE'S SCARY!

PROFESSOR MINUSCULE
HEAD OF THE FACT CAVE AND
THE BRAINS BEHIND MISSIONS

FACTORELLA
PROFESSOR MINUSCULE'S
DAUGHTER AND ALL-AROUND
WHIZ KID

CHAPTER 1
MONKEY IN SPACE!

It was a typical day for TV's worst weatherman, Cliff Thornhill. He was in the Boss's office getting yelled at—again!

"Yesterday you said it was going to snow!" screamed the Boss. "But it was sunny! You never get the weather right!"

Luckily for Cliff and Puddles, Cliff's copresenter and canine companion, the audience loved them.

So, even if they did always get the weather wrong, the Boss couldn't fire them.

As they returned to their office after meeting with the Boss, Cliff and Puddles noticed a huge crowd gathered around a TV screen.

"There's a monkey on a collision course with Mars!" gasped Lucy, Cliff's friend from the Makeup department.

"A monkey in space?" Cliff asked.

"It's not just any monkey," explained Lucy. "That's Dr. Barnabas, the world's most intelligent primate. He's on a mission to explore Mars, and his spaceship, Ape-ollo 13, has been damaged. He's down to his last two bananas. He can't last much longer!"

Before Lucy could even finish her sentence, Cliff and Puddles had taken off.

Strange, thought Lucy. Cliff and Puddles always seem to disappear whenever there's a crisis. . . .

Slightly out of breath, Cliff and Puddles reached their office.

"Cliff, you know what this is. . . ." said Puddles excitedly. Puddles spoke only when he was alone with Cliff.

"Yes," said Cliff quite dramatically. "This is a . . ."

"Stop right there!" shouted Puddles. "It's my turn to say it."

"You always say it," whined Cliff.

"Pleeeeease . . ." Puddles said.

"Oh, all right. But I'm saying it next time," said Cliff.

5

And with that, Puddles pulled a lever. The portrait of Cliff's great-great-great-uncle Sir Phineas Thornhill began to shake and then slowly slid back to reveal a secret tunnel. . . .

CREAK!

WHIRR!

"All right, Puddles—uh, I mean, Knowledge—we've got a long journey ahead of us," Captain Fact said as they ran through the corridors of the Fact Cave.

"I like long trips," said Knowledge, breathing hard. "Should I pack my bathing suit?"

"Don't be silly. We're going to Mars to rescue Dr. Barnabas," Captain Fact said.

"Great! Where do we catch the bus? Or do we take a train?" asked Knowledge.

"That's a ridiculous thought, Knowledge. We need a spaceship! One with plenty of room for bananas . . . We've got a monkey to rescue!"

"But why is the monkey in space, anyway?" asked Knowledge as they reached the door to the Fact Cave's Nerve Center.

"**KER-FACT!** Monkeys have been sent into space for years," said Captain Fact. "The first monkey in space was named Gordo, back in 1958!"

"But why were they sent?" Knowledge asked.

"It was to see whether it was possible to live in outer space. Now animals help out on all sorts of experiments. Hold on to your Fact Mask, Knowledge. I feel a Fact Attack coming on," said Captain Fact, as his head began to throb. . . .

14

"Oh," Knowledge sighed. "I thought I was going to be the first dog in space."

"Well," said Captain Fact, "you'll be the first *weather*dog in space."

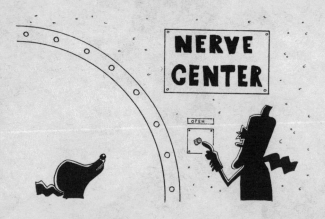

"Great!" Knowledge said. "But where are we going to find a spaceship to take us there?"

CHAPTER 2
COUNTDOWN

"**A**h, Captain Fact and Knowledge, there you two are. What took you so long?" asked Professor Minuscule, the world's shortest genius. While Captain Fact and Knowledge forecast the weather as Cliff and Puddles, Professor Minuscule worked in the Fact Cave, planning missions and inventing fact-astic gadgets.

"Getting to Mars isn't going to be easy," warned Professor Minuscule. "But I've invented the supercharged, extra-boosted FactNik #1. It should get you there in time to rescue Dr. Barnabas."

Just then, Factorella, Professor
Minuscule's daughter, rushed in wearing
a brand-new spacesuit.

"When do we leave, Dad?" Factorella
asked enthusiastically.

"How many times do I have to tell you?
You're too young to go on missions,"
Professor Minuscule scolded. "You have to
wait until you're older."

"But you're always sending me out to
rescue Captain Fact and Knowledge when
they're in trouble," moaned Factorella.

"That's part of your training," said
Professor Minuscule, "and so is being in
charge of the computers. What have you
come up with on space travel?"

"Tons," Factorella said. She fired up the Fact Cave's supercomputer, which was known as Factotum.

SPACE IS A DANGEROUS PLACE—DUST TRAVELS FASTER THAN BULLETS!

SPACE STARTS 621.37 MILES ABOVE THE EARTH.

MARS IS 48 MILLION MILES FROM EARTH. AN ORDINARY SPACESHIP WOULD TAKE SEVEN MONTHS TO GET THERE!

NO MAN (OR DOG) HAS EVER BEEN TO MARS.

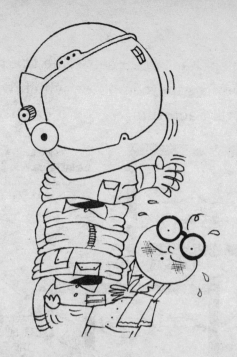

"Don't we have a weather forecast to do?" asked Knowledge, who was beginning to get cold paws.

"I'll go!" shouted Factorella.

"No," said Professor Minuscule. "Don't you have to debug Factotum?"

"I guess so," Factorella said, with a sigh.

"Come on, Knowledge," said Captain Fact. "Think of Dr. Barnabas—the weather can wait."

"There's no time to waste. Put on these
protective space suits. You'll need them for
takeoff and landing. I've never made one
for a dog before—it was quite a challenge,"
said Professor Minuscule, as he handed
Captain Fact and Knowledge their outfits.

"I like the badge," said Knowledge.

"**KER-FACT!** All space expeditions have a specially designed cloth badge, called a mission badge," said Captain Fact.

Professor Minuscule shoved them toward the exit. "We must hurry to the launchpad. Your spaceship is ready for takeoff."

"You'll find a toolbox full of gadgets in the cockpit for when you get closer to Mars," said Professor Minuscule. "And a big bag of bananas for Dr. Barnabas."

As they approached the spaceship, Captain Fact's nose began to twitch. He was about to have a . . .

FACT

FACT
THE SPACE SHUTTLE, FIRST LAUNCHED
IN 1981, WAS THE FIRST REUSABLE SPACECRAFT.
IT LANDS LIKE A PLANE!

SPACECRAFT

FACT
AT BLASTOFF, ROCKETS CAN REACH
TEMPERATURES OF UP TO 5,972° F. THAT'S
TWICE THE TEMPERATURE THAT MELTS
STEEL!

Captain Fact and Knowledge nervously climbed aboard the spaceship. After a few last-minute checks, it would be liftoff!

SECRET FACT!

(Shhh! Don't tell!)

HOW COME CAPTAIN FACT KNOWS SO MUCH?

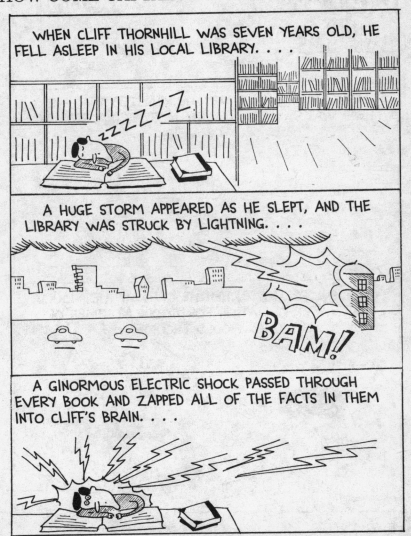

WHEN CLIFF THORNHILL WAS SEVEN YEARS OLD, HE FELL ASLEEP IN HIS LOCAL LIBRARY. . . .

A HUGE STORM APPEARED AS HE SLEPT, AND THE LIBRARY WAS STRUCK BY LIGHTNING. . . .

BAM!

A GINORMOUS ELECTRIC SHOCK PASSED THROUGH EVERY BOOK AND ZAPPED ALL OF THE FACTS IN THEM INTO CLIFF'S BRAIN. . . .

(NOW, BACK TO THE STORY . . .)

CHAPTER 3

5
4
3
2
1

BLASTOFF!

As their spaceship, FactNik #1, took off, Captain Fact and Knowledge began to feel very strange.

"Wait, what's going on? I feel all weird and wobbly, and my tail's throbbing," Knowledge said. "I wonder if it was that minestrone–flavored dog biscuit I had for breakfast."

"No, it's the extreme speed," replied Captain Fact.

"But my head feels like a big, blown-up balloon!" shrieked Knowledge.

"That's because right now, all your fluids are rushing to your head. On Earth,

gravity pulls the body's fluids down towards the toes," explained Captain Fact.

"I'm not sure if I'm cut out for this astronaut business," said Knowledge. "I prefer a nice, warm TV studio. How do astronauts do this?"

"Unlike us, they have had years of training," said Captain Fact.

"Really?" asked Knowledge. "You mean, there's an astronaut school?"

Just then, Captain Fact started to shudder. He was having another . . .

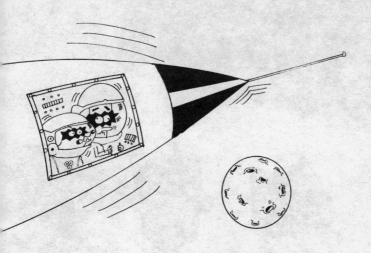

FACT

ASTRONAUT TRAINING

1. IF YOU WANT TO BECOME AN ASTRONAUT IT WILL TAKE AT LEAST TWO YEARS OF TOUGH TRAINING.

2. YOU HAVE TO LEARN HOW TO SURVIVE AT SEA, BECAUSE SPACECRAFTS OFTEN LAND IN THE WATER.

3. THE MOVEMENT SIMULATOR HELPS YOU GET USED TO FLOATING.

$\pi = 3.174$

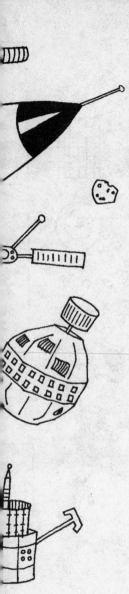

After they were safely in space, Captain Fact took the controls and started to fly the spaceship all the way to Mars.

"This looks easy," said Knowledge. "Space is empty—there are no traffic lights, no cars, no people. Can I try to drive?"

"Well, you're wrong about space being empty," said Captain Fact as he handed the controls to Knowledge. "Look out the window. Space is full of stuff—rocks, dust, satellites. **KER-FACT!** There are at least 1,000 working satellites zooming around the earth.

"And we're heading for one right now!" he added, trying to stay calm as he grabbed back the controls. "I'll steer. You make contact with Dr. Barnabas."

Knowledge tweaked the dials and fiddled with the buttons, and eventually a crackly picture popped up on the video screen.

". . . *Fizzzz*—come in, please—*crackle*—I'm off course—*pop*—fuel low, banana levels critical—*crackle*—are you receiving me?"

"Did you hear that, Captain Fact? Banana levels are critical—hit the boosters!"

Captain Fact and Knowledge got the spaceship up to top speed. Avoiding satellites, they began the longest and most dangerous part of their journey—flying beyond the moon to Mars.

"There's still about 48 million miles to go," said Captain Fact. "It's going to take a while, so you'd better get used to living in space, Knowledge. In the meantime, Factorella has provided us with Factotum's Fact File on all of the planets."

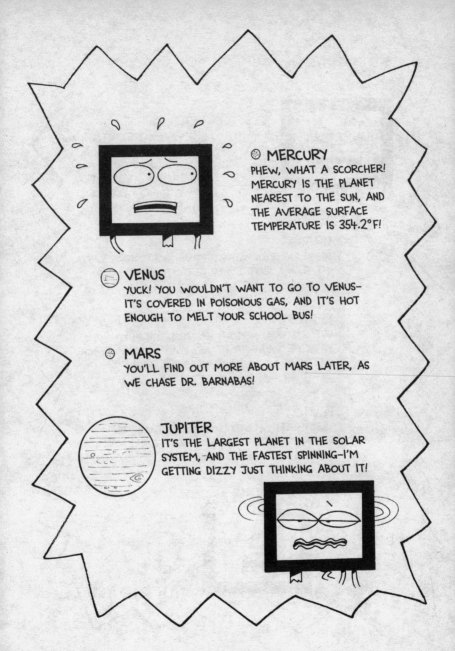

⊙ MERCURY

PHEW, WHAT A SCORCHER! MERCURY IS THE PLANET NEAREST TO THE SUN, AND THE AVERAGE SURFACE TEMPERATURE IS 354.2°F!

⊙ VENUS

YUCK! YOU WOULDN'T WANT TO GO TO VENUS—IT'S COVERED IN POISONOUS GAS, AND IT'S HOT ENOUGH TO MELT YOUR SCHOOL BUS!

⊙ MARS

YOU'LL FIND OUT MORE ABOUT MARS LATER, AS WE CHASE DR. BARNABAS!

JUPITER

IT'S THE LARGEST PLANET IN THE SOLAR SYSTEM, AND THE FASTEST SPINNING—I'M GETTING DIZZY JUST THINKING ABOUT IT!

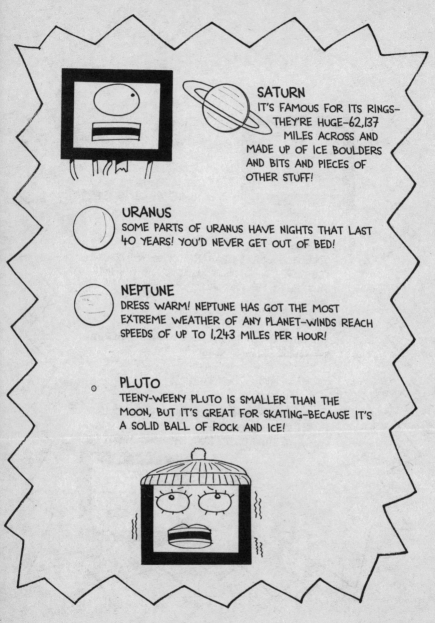

SATURN
IT'S FAMOUS FOR ITS RINGS—THEY'RE HUGE—62,137 MILES ACROSS AND MADE UP OF ICE BOULDERS AND BITS AND PIECES OF OTHER STUFF!

URANUS
SOME PARTS OF URANUS HAVE NIGHTS THAT LAST 40 YEARS! YOU'D NEVER GET OUT OF BED!

NEPTUNE
DRESS WARM! NEPTUNE HAS GOT THE MOST EXTREME WEATHER OF ANY PLANET—WINDS REACH SPEEDS OF UP TO 1,243 MILES PER HOUR!

PLUTO
TEENY-WEENY PLUTO IS SMALLER THAN THE MOON, BUT IT'S GREAT FOR SKATING—BECAUSE IT'S A SOLID BALL OF ROCK AND ICE!

CHAPTER 4

POWDERED PINEAPPLE

They'd been in space for only half an hour when Knowledge said, "I'm hungry. Can we stop somewhere for lunch?"

"There aren't any restaurants in space, Knowledge," said Captain Fact. "But don't worry. Professor Minuscule has provided us with some wonderful space food."

"Excellent!" said Knowledge. "I'll have a chili–flavored dog biscuit covered in gravy and a strawberry one for dessert."

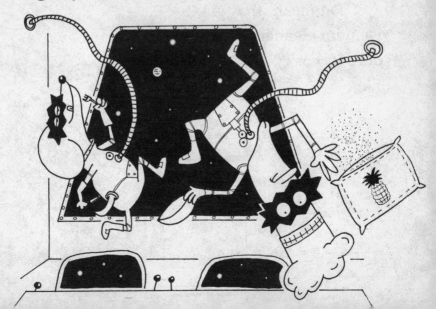

"I'm afraid that we don't have that," said Captain Fact. "**KER-FACT!** Everything you eat in space has to be specially packaged. Try some of this dried pear and powdered pineapple. Yum!"

"Yuck! I think I'll wait until we get back to Earth," said Knowledge. "I'm going to go to the little dog's room. Is it through here?"

"No! Don't open that! That's the emergency escape hatch! The toilet's over there."

"You mean, that giant vacuum cleaner? How does it work?"

SNIFF
SNIFF

"Let me explain," said Captain Fact. "You need some Space-Toilet Facts. Because of weightlessness, a conventional toilet would lead to all sorts of things floating around. And you wouldn't want to bump into any of that, would you? Basically, the toilet is a giant vacuum cleaner—it sucks everything up. Your pee is even recycled into drinking water and oxygen!"

"I think I've heard quite enough on space toilets," said Knowledge. He was starting to feel a bit queasy.

"Living in space is nothing like living on the earth," said Captain Fact as his nose began to tingle.

It was time for a . . .

". . . *Crackle*—Fact Cave calling
FactNik #1; come in, please: this is
Professor Minuscule calling!"

"Good," Knowledge said. "I wanted to
have a word with you. This space food—it's
horrible! Is there any chance you could
send up some dog biscuits? And as for the
space toilet . . ."

"There's no time for that—*fizz*—you're
on a collision course with a meteor!"

CHAPTER 5

BUMP!

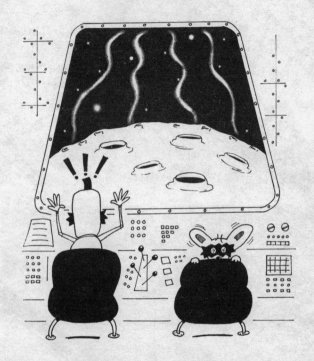

"**B**uckle up, Knowledge! This could get bumpy," warned Captain Fact as he sat down in his seat.

"What's a meteor?" asked Knowledge.

Captain Fact's ears began to wobble and he prepared himself for another . . .

"We've been knocked miles off course. All of our communications systems are out of order," said Captain Fact. He was busy dusting himself off after hitting the meteor.

"I'm beginning to understand how
Dr. Barnabas must feel," Knowledge said.
"At least we've got plenty of bananas. . . ."

"Don't even think about eating those.
We're on a mission here, and we're not
going to fail. We've just got to get out of
this pickle first," said Captain Fact.

Whenever Captain Fact and Knowledge found themselves in a pickle they used one of Professor Minuscule's most ingenious inventions: the Fact Watch. Now, Captain Fact pressed the emergency button and Professor Minuscule appeared on the watch face.

"Minuscule, we have a problem," said Captain Fact.

"I know," said the professor. "I've been tracking your progress, and I've sent Factorella."

HELP IS ON THE WAY!

Suddenly, FactNik #1 began to shudder, and then there was a huge bang. Knowledge looked out the window. . . .

"There's a spaceship coming straight for us!" he cried.

In a flash, Factorella appeared.

"Wow! This is great!" she said.

"Space is fantastic! Now, Dad's told me exactly what to do. I'm going to tow you to the nearest space station to get the ship repaired. Knowledge, you like going on walks, don't you?"

"Yes," replied Knowledge, who actually preferred eating barbecue–flavored dog biscuits.

"Get your space suit on," Factorella said. "You're going for a space walk. I need you to tie this rope to the front of your ship."

"**KER-FACT!** Work outside a spaceship is called 'extravehicular activity,'" said Captain Fact as Knowledge prepared to leave FactNik #1.

And so, Knowledge became the first dog ever to walk in space. When he'd attached the rope, Factorella was able to pull their broken-down spaceship through the asteroid belt to a nearby space station.

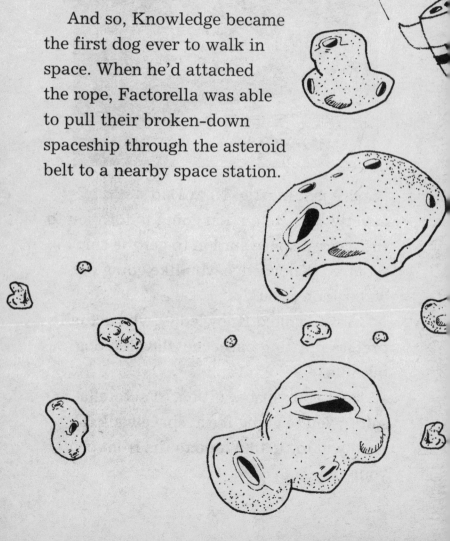

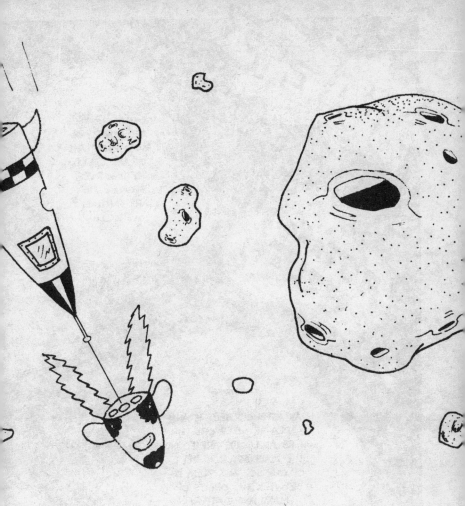

As they passed through the
asteroid belt, Captain Fact's
toes began to tingle as he felt
another . . .

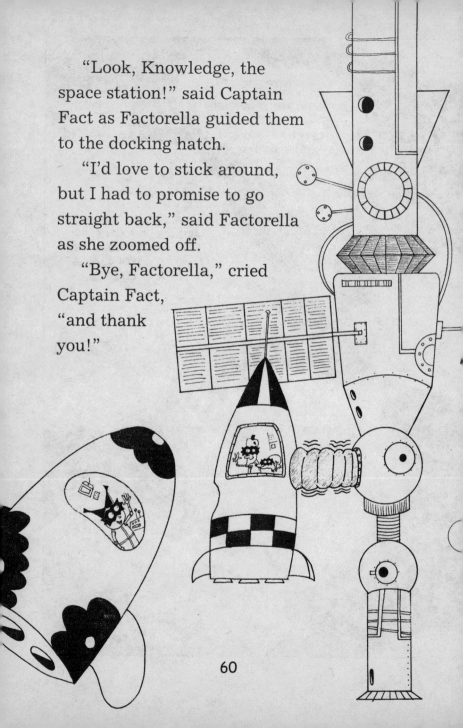

"Look, Knowledge, the space station!" said Captain Fact as Factorella guided them to the docking hatch.

"I'd love to stick around, but I had to promise to go straight back," said Factorella as she zoomed off.

"Bye, Factorella," cried Captain Fact, "and thank you!"

CHAPTER 6

BORIS

As Captain Fact and Knowledge, now dressed in their superhero outfits, boarded the space station, a very large, unshaven cosmonaut greeted them. He scooped both Captain Fact and Knowledge up in a huge bear hug.

"Hello, hello! I'm Cosmonaut Boris, and I'm so delighted to see you! You are my first visitors in three years!"

"I can't breathe!" wheezed Knowledge.

"You're squashing my cape," gasped Captain Fact.

"Professor Minuscule has told me about your encounter with a meteor. It shouldn't take long to repair the ship," said Boris. "It will make a nice change from doing endless experiments. That's all I do out here—eat, sleep, and conduct experiments. . . ."

"We've never been on a space station before," said Knowledge, straightening his squished cape.

As Boris got to work repairing FactNik #1, Captain Fact and Knowledge explored.

"It's like being in a giant train," said Knowledge.

"It's a bit more complicated than that, Knowledge," said Captain Fact as his knees began to tremble and he was struck by a . . .

"Your ship is repaired and ready to go—I've even added extra boosters!" said Boris. "Are you sure you can't stick around? I get so lonely all on my own up here. We could play chess, listen to music . . . I've even got some powdered cabbage!"

"Sorry, Cosmonaut Boris, but we really must go," Knowledge said.

"We can't leave Dr. Barnabas waiting any longer," Captain Fact told him.

"I understand. Good luck! And if you're ever near the space station, don't be a stranger."

Without further ado, Captain Fact and Knowledge fired up FactNik #1.

LET GO OF MY CAPE!

CHAPTER 7

DESTINATION: MARS

Once again, Captain Fact and Knowledge were hurtling through space toward Mars.

". . . *Crackle*—Professor Minuscule here—*fizz*—come in, FactNik #1!"

"FactNik #1 here," replied Captain Fact.

". . . *Crackle*—with those incredibly powerful boosters that Cosmonaut Boris fitted—*pop*—you should be approaching Mars shortly."

"At last . . . Mars," said Captain Fact as the tip of his nose began to twitch and he launched into a . . .

As Captain Fact and Knowledge got closer to Mars, a small dot appeared on the radar. It was getting bigger every second. . . ."It's Ape-ollo 13! We're going to save Dr. Barnabas!" Knowledge cried.

"Not so fast, Knowledge," said Captain Fact. "I think he's about to . . .

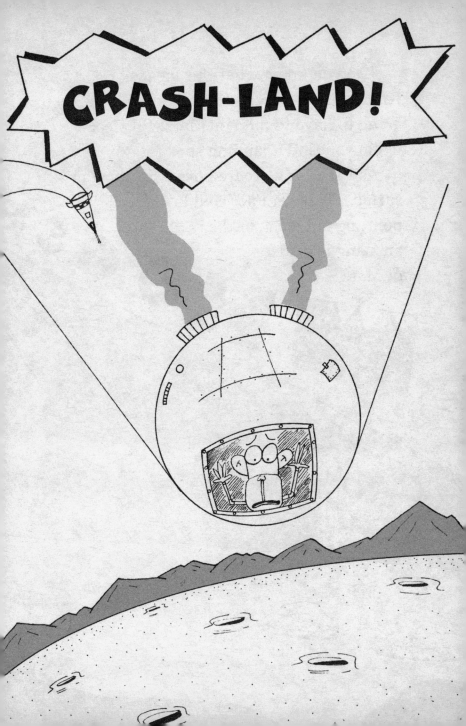

"Do you know what this means, Knowledge?" Captain Fact said. "We're going to have to land on Mars! I'll steer while you find a landing spot."

As FactNik #1 roared over the Martian surface, Captain Fact couldn't resist pointing out some of the amazing features of Mars.

WHOOSH

At last they found a safe place to land.
"Great landing spot, Knowledge!" said
Captain Fact.

"There's just one problem," replied
Knowledge, peering at the instruments,
"Dr. Barnabas is over a mile away!"

CHAPTER 8

GOING BANANAS

"All right, then. Space suits on. There's no time to waste," Captain Fact said, reaching into Professor Minuscule's box of gadgets.

"Wouldn't it be quicker without these bulky suits?" asked Knowledge. "They weigh a ton."

"You can't walk around a place as inhospitable as Mars without a space suit on!" Captain Fact said. His earlobes began to wobble and he felt the beginning of a . . .

After twenty minutes of staggering and stumbling across Mars's rocky surface, Captain Fact and Knowledge were getting nowhere fast.

"We're never going to reach Dr. Barnabas in time," sighed Knowledge. "I can barely move in this thing. Isn't there a gadget in Professor Minuscule's toolbox that could speed things up?"

"I'll take a look," said Captain Fact, waddling back to FactNik #1. After rummaging around, he emerged with a space vehicle. "**KER-FACT!** The Sojourner

robot buggy was specially designed to
explore the surface of Mars, and it travels
at 1.3 feet per minute. Luckily, this one's
been turbocharged by Professor Minuscule.
We'll get to Dr. Barnabas in no time," he
said, jumping on board.

As they set off, Captain Fact noticed
that Knowledge was covering his eyes.

"I'm worried we might meet some little
green men," Knowledge whispered.

"You've been reading too much science
fiction," said Captain Fact as his chin
began to wobble and he felt the beginning
of another . . .

With their vehicle moving at top speed, Captain Fact and Knowledge soon saw Dr. Barnabas.

"Hang on, Dr. Barnabas, we're coming!" shouted Captain Fact. "And we've got bananas!"

And so, after a death-defying journey,
Captain Fact and Knowledge finally
reached Dr. Barnabas. . . .

"It's great to see you! I knew you'd make it! Mmmm . . ." said Dr. Barnabas, as he chewed on his fifteenth banana.

"There's no time to waste," said Captain Fact urgently. "We're starting to run out of oxygen—we've got to get back to Earth!"

CHAPTER 9

MONKEY ON BOARD

With the world's most intelligent primate firmly strapped into his seat, Captain Fact and Knowledge blasted off from Mars and began the descent to Earth.

"We'll have you back in no time, Dr. Barnabas," said Captain Fact. "All we have to do is avoid the satellites, asteroids, and meteors we ran into on the way here."

"Speaking of space junk, look at the size of that piece of rubble," said Knowledge.

"That's not space junk, that's the moon," explained Captain Fact. His nostrils were twitching again, and he got ready for a . . .

"We're heading straight for it!" screamed Dr. Barnabas.

"Hit the brakes!" shouted Captain Fact, pulling back on his control stick as hard as he could.

REVERSE THRUSTERS TO MAXIMUM!!!

At the last second, FactNik #1 screeched away from the moon's surface.

"That was close!" said Knowledge, gently helping Dr. Barnabas back into his seat.

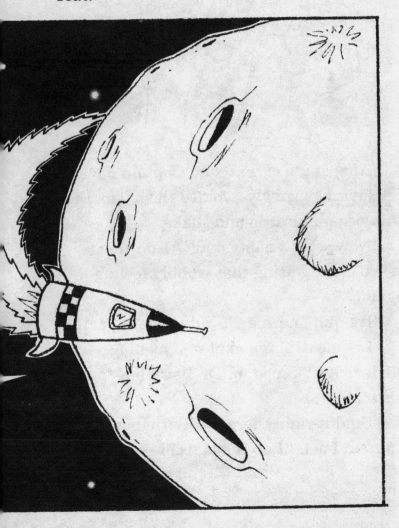

"Almost too close," said Captain Fact.

Having narrowly avoided the moon, the ship began to rattle and shake.

"Now what's happening?" Knowledge asked. "I'm getting that wobbly feeling again!"

"It's quite normal," said Captain Fact.

"Let me explain what's happening, Knowledge," piped up Dr. Barnabas from his seat.

"Hold it right there, Dr. Barnabas!" said Captain Fact. "*I* do the facts around here.

KER-FACT! We're reentering the earth's atmosphere, which means that the ship's under a huge amount of pressure. That's why you're feeling so strange, Knowledge."

". . . *Crackle*—FactNik #1, this is Professor Minuscule—*fizz*—you're coming in for a landing—*crackle*—you'll need to splash down in water."

"We're over the Pacific," Dr. Barnabas said. "I know a great island we could land near—beautiful beaches, glorious sunsets, and all the bananas you can eat!"

"There's no time for that, Dr. Barnabas," said Captain Fact as he clutched the controls of the shaking spaceship. "We've got an evening weather forecast to present. We have to land near home."

CHAPTER 10

AND NOW, THE WEATHER . . .

"**W**hat about the city pool?" said
Knowledge.

"It's an *indoor* pool," replied Captain
Fact.

"How about the aquarium?" suggested
Dr. Barnabas.

"That's got sharks," said Captain Fact.

"The park!" exclaimed Knowledge.

"Good idea! It's got a pond," said
Captain Fact. "We'll land there!"

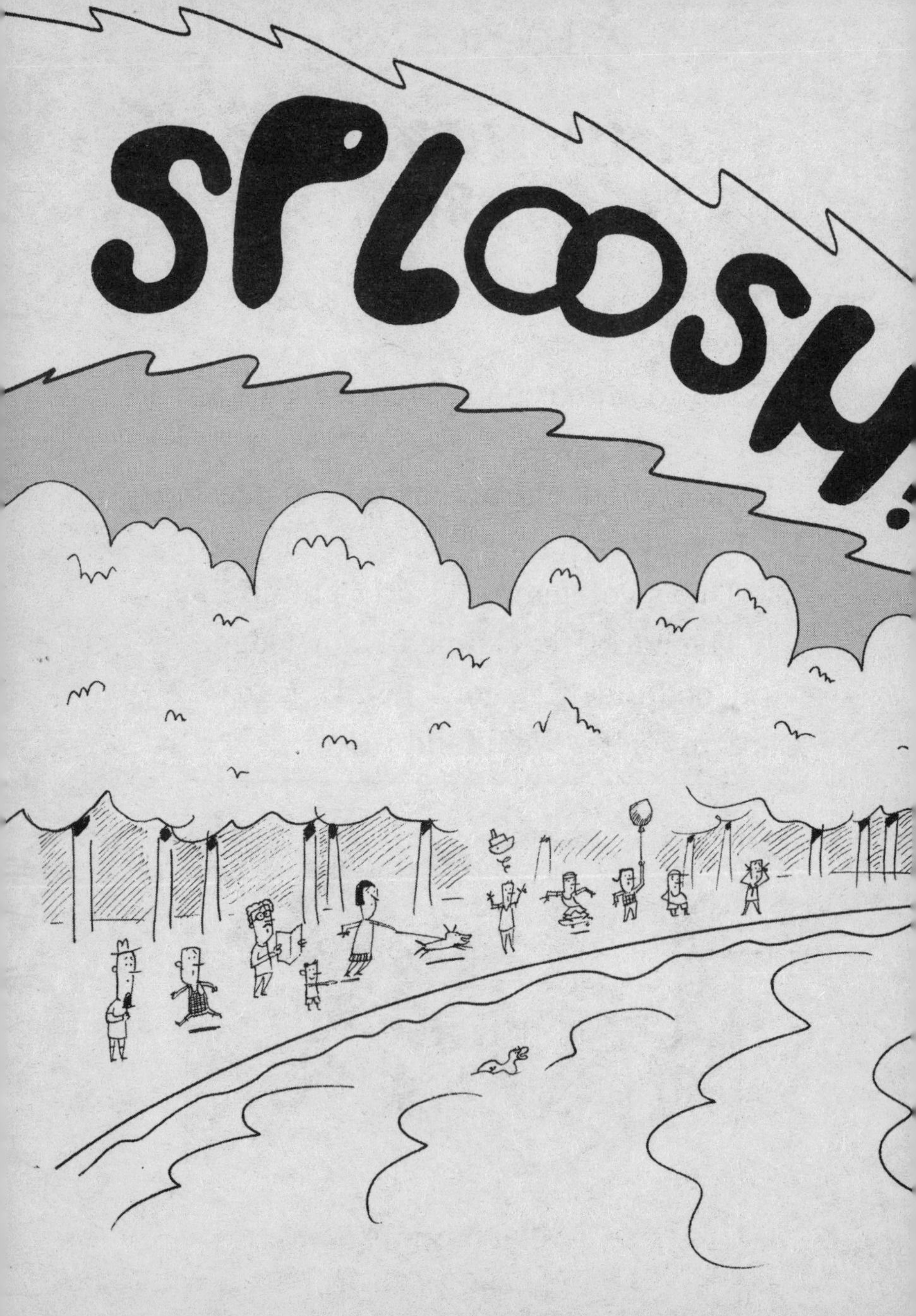
SPLOOSH!

"We did it!" shouted Captain Fact, as the spaceship bobbed to the surface.

"Home at last," said Knowledge. "I can't wait to get some real food—chocolate peanut–flavored dog biscuits, here I come!"

"Thank you, Captain Fact and Knowledge," said Dr. Barnabas. "I'm on a mission to Saturn next week. You should come along."

"I think we'll be staying on Earth, thank you, Dr. Barnabas," said Captain Fact. Just then he realized that a huge crowd had gathered. "We'd better sneak away. Our identities must remain a secret," he said.

Captain Fact and Knowledge didn't have time to get changed as they rushed into the TV studio. In fact, they only just had time to take their masks off.

"We made it!" said Captain Fact as he crashed right into the Boss.

"Where on earth have you been? And why are you wearing those ridiculous space suits?" demanded the Boss.

"We were just at a . . . er . . . um . . . a costume party!" Captain Fact blurted out.

"Well, it's one minute to six. Get changed and get over to the studio. NOW!" screamed the Boss.

Pulling their space suits off as they ran down the corridors of the TV studio, Captain Fact and Knowledge burst through the doors of the Makeup department.

"Ah, Cliff and Puddles, there you are," said Lucy. "Did you hear the exciting

news? Dr. Barnabas was rescued!"

"Really?" said Cliff, pretending not to know anything about it. "Who rescued him?"

"Captain Fact and Knowledge," said Lucy dreamily. "I'd love to meet Captain Fact. He's my hero."

"Er . . . um . . ." said Cliff, blushing.

"Come on, Cliff," whispered Puddles.

"We've got the weather to do."

And so, with Dr. Barnabas safely back on Earth, Cliff Thornhill and Puddles were back to doing what they did worst—the weather.

Until the next crisis . . .

KNIFE & PACKER FACT!

WHEN KNIFE AND PACKER WERE GROWING UP THEY DREAMED OF ONE DAY GOING INTO SPACE. BUT BY THE TIME THEY WERE OLD ENOUGH TO BE ASTRONAUTS, THEY COULDN'T SQUEEZE INTO THEIR SPACE SUITS! SO INSTEAD, THEY'VE BEEN WRITING AND DRAWING TOGETHER EVER SINCE.